In this brilliant tale which takes the form of a letter to a girl called Jane, the unnamed main character, a man much like James himself, a studious and quiet gentleman, tells of his strange experiences recently.

His five senses *have* been behaving oddly lately - he begins to hear whispering words in the rush of a stream; stopping for a rest, he dreams of a strange plant growing between tree roots in a wood through which the stream runs. On waking, and led by the stream's whispering, he finds that the place and the plant are indeed real. He eats part of it, and a very peculiar thing happens - suddenly he can see under the ground! Astonished and fascinated, he walks on. To his amazement, his new deeper vision enables him to spy, buried a few inches beneath the surface, a mysterious metallic box. Intrigued, he digs it up, but it seems completely sealed.

Late that night, back in his room, just when the moon shines directly onto the box, cracks appear! Inside are five jars, with odd ancient writing on them giving tantalizing hints of what their contents might be able to do . . .

THE FIVE JARS

BEING MORE OR LESS OF A FAIRY TALE
CONTAINED IN A LETTER
TO A YOUNG PERSON

~ by the same author ~

Ghost Stories of an Antiquary (1904)
More Ghost Stories of an Antiquary (1911)
A Thin Ghost (1919)
The Five Jars (1922)
A Warning to the Curious (1925)

THE BAT-BALL

[*See page* 135.

THE FIVE JARS

BEING MORE OR LESS OF A FAIRY TALE
CONTAINED IN A LETTER
TO A YOUNG PERSON

by

M.R. JAMES

illustrated by
GILBERT JAMES

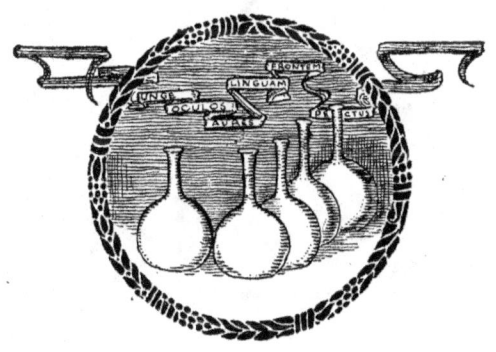

ADELAIDE
MICHAEL WALMER
2013

The Five Jars first published 1922
This edition published 2013

by

Michael Walmer
49 Second Street
Gawler South
South Australia 5118

ISBN 978-0-9873678-2-2 paperback
ISBN 978-0-9873678-3-9 ebook

CONTENTS

LIST OF ILLUSTRATIONS

THE DISCOVERY

I

THE DISCOVERY

MY DEAR JANE,

You remember that you were puzzled when I told you I had heard something from the owls—or if not puzzled (for I know you have some experience of these things), you were at any rate anxious to know exactly how it happened. Perhaps the time has now come for you to be told.

It was really luck, and not any skill of mine, that put me in the way of it; luck, and also being ready to believe more than I could see. I have promised not to put down on paper the name of the wood where it happened: that can keep till we meet; but all the rest I can tell exactly as it came about.

It is a wood with a stream at the edge of it; the water is brown and clear. On the other side of it are flat meadows, and beyond these a hillside quite covered with an oak wood. The stream has alder-trees along it, and is pretty well shaded over; the sun hits it in places and makes flecks of light through the leaves.

The day I am thinking of was a very hot one in early September. I had come across the meadows with some idea of sitting by the stream and reading. The only change in my plans that I made was that instead of sitting down I lay down, and instead of reading I went to sleep.

You know how sometimes—but very, very seldom—you see something in a dream which you are quite sure is real. So it was with me this time. I did not dream any story or see any people; I only dreamt of a plant. In the dream no one told me anything about it: I just saw it growing under a tree: a small bit of the tree root came into the picture, an old gnarled root covered with moss, and with three sorts of eyes in it, round holes trimmed with moss—you know the kind. The plant was not one I should have thought much about, though certainly it was not one that I knew: it had no flowers or berries, and grew quite squat in the ground; more like a yellow aconite without the flower than anything else. It seemed to consist of a ring of six leaves spread out pretty flat with nine points on each leaf. As I say, I saw this quite clearly, and remembered it because six times nine makes fifty-four, which happens to be a number which I had a particular reason for remembering at that moment.

Well, there was no more in the dream than that: but, such as it was, it fixed itself in my mind like a photograph, and I was sure that if ever I saw that tree root and that plant, I should know them again. And, though I neither saw nor heard anything more of them than I have told you, it was borne in upon my mind that the plant *was* worth finding.

When I woke up I still lay, feeling very lazy, on the grass with my head within a foot or two of the edge of the stream and listened to its noise, until in five or six minutes—whether I began to doze off again or not does not much matter—the water-sound became like words, and said, " *Trickle-up, trickle-up,*" an immense number of times. It pleased me, for though in poetry we hear a deal about babbling brooks, and though I am particularly fond of the noise they make, I never was able before to pretend that I could hear any words. And when I did finally get up and shake myself awake I thought I would anyhow pay so much attention to what the water said as to stroll up the stream instead of down. So I did : it took me through the flat meadows, but still along the edge of the wood, and still every now and then I heard the same peculiar noise which sounded like *Trickle-up.*

Not so very long after, I came to a place where another stream ran out of the wood into the one I had been following, and just below the place where the two joined there was—not a bridge, but a pole across, and another pole to serve as a rail, by which you could cross, without trouble. I did cross, not thinking much about it, but with some idea of looking at this new little stream, which went at a very quick pace and seemed to promise small rapids and waterfalls a little higher up. Now when I got to the edge of it, there was no mistake: it was saying "*Trickle-up*," or even "*Track-up*," much plainer than the old one. I stepped across it and went a few yards up the old stream. Before the new one joined it, it was saying nothing of the kind. I went back to the new one: it was talking as plain as print. Of course there were no two words about what must be done now. Here was something quite new, and even if I missed my tea, it had got to be looked into. So I went up the new stream into the wood.

Though I was well on the look-out for unusual things—in particular the plant, which I could not help thinking about—I cannot say there was anything peculiar about the stream or the plants or the insects or the trees (except the words which the water kept saying) so long as I was in the flat part of the wood. But soon I came to a steepish bank—the land began to slope up suddenly and the rapids and waterfalls of the brook were very gay and interesting. Then, besides *Track-up*, which was now its word always instead of *Trickle*, I heard every now and then *All right*, which was encouraging and exciting. Still, there was nothing out of the way to be seen, look as I might.

The climb up the slope or bank was fairly long. At the top was a kind of terrace, pretty level and with large old trees growing upon it, mainly oaks. Behind there was a further slope up and still more wood-land : but that does not matter now. For the present I was at the end of my wander-ings. There was no more stream, and I had found what of all natural things I think pleases me best, a real spring of water quite untouched.

Five or six oaks grew in something like a semicircle, and in the middle of the flat ground in front of them was an almost per-fectly round pool, not more than four or five feet across. The bottom of it in the middle was pale sand which was continually rising up in little egg-shaped mounds and fall-ing down again. It was the clearest and strongest spring of the kind I had ever seen, and I could have watched it for hours. I did sit down by it and watch it for some time without thinking of anything but the luck I had had to find it. But then I began to wonder if it would say anything. Naturally I could not expect it to say " *Track-up* " any more, for here I was at the

2

end of it. So I listened with some curiosity. It hardly made so much noise as the stream : the pool was deeper. But I thought it must say something, and I put my head down as close as I could to the surface of the water. If I am not mistaken (and as things turned out I am sure I was right) the words were : *Gather gather, pick pick,* or *quick quick.*

Now I had not been thinking about the plant for a little time ; but, as you may suppose, this brought it back to my mind and I got up and began to look about at the roots of the old oaks which grew just round the spring. No, none of the roots on this side which faced towards the water were like that which I had seen—still, the feeling was strong upon me that this, if any, was the kind of place, and even the very place, where the plant must be. So I walked to the back of the trees, being careful to go from right to left, according to the course of the sun.

Well, I was not mistaken. At the back of the middlemost oak-tree there were the roots I had dreamt of with the moss and the holes like eyes, and between them was the plant. I think the only thing which was new to me in the look of it was that it was so extraordinarily *green*. It seemed to have in it all the greenness that was possible or that would be wanted for a whole field of grass.

I had some scruples about touching it. In fact, I actually went back to the spring and listened, to make sure that it was still saying the same thing. Yes, it was: "*Gather gather, pick.*" But there was something else every now and then which I could *not* for the life of me make out at first. I lay down, put my hand round my ear and held my breath. It might have been *bark tree* or *dark tree* or *cask free.* I got impatient at last and said:

"Well, I'm very sorry, but do what I will I *cannot* make out what you are trying to say."

Instantly a little spirt of water hit me on the ear, and I heard, as clear as possible, what it was : " *Ask tree.*"

I got up at once. " I *beg* your pardon," I said, " of course. Thank you very much ; " and the water went on saying " *Gather gather, all right, dip dip.*"

After thinking how best to greet it, I went back to the oak, stood in front of it and said (of course baring my head) :

" Oak, I humbly desire your good leave to gather the green plant which grows between your roots. If an acorn falls into this my right hand " (which I held out) " I will count it that you answer yes—and give you thanks." The acorn fell straight into the palm of my hand. I said, " I thank you, Oak : good growth to you. I will lay this your acorn in the place whence I gather the plant."

Then very carefully I took hold of the stalk of the plant (which was very short, for, as I said, it grew rather flat on the ground) and pulled, and to my surprise it came up as easily as a mushroom. It had a clean round bulb without any rootlets and left a smooth neat hole in the ground, in which, according to promise, I laid the acorn, and covered it in with earth. I think it very likely that it will turn into a second plant.

Then I remembered the last word of the spring and went back to dip the plant in it. I had a shock when I did so, and it was lucky I was holding it firm, for when it touched the water it struggled in my hand like a fish or a newt and almost slipped out. I dipped it three times and thought I felt it growing smaller in my hand : and indeed when I looked at it I found it had shut up its leaves and curled them in quite close, so that the whole thing was little more than a bulb. As I looked at it I thought the water changed its note and said, " *That'll do, that'll do.*"

I thought it was time to thank the spring for all it had done for me, though, as you may suppose, I did not yet know in the least what was to be done with the plant, or what use it was going to be.

So I went over and said in the politest words I could how much I was obliged, and if there was anything I had or could do which would be agreeable, how glad I should be. Then I listened carefully, for it seemed by this time quite natural that I should get some sort of answer. It came. There was a sudden change in the sound, and the water said clearly and rapidly, "*Silver silver silver silver.*" I felt in my pocket. Luckily I had several shillings, sixpences and half-crowns. I thought the best way was to offer them all, so I put them in the palm of my right hand and held it under the water, open, just over the dancing sand. For a few seconds the water ran over the silver without doing anything: only the coins seemed to grow very bright and clean. Then one of the shillings was very neatly and smoothly slid off, and then another and a sixpence. I waited, but no more happened, and the water seemed to draw itself down and away from my hand, and to say " *All right.*" So I got up.

The three coins lay on the bottom of the pool looking brighter than even the newest I have ever seen, and gradually as they lay there they began to appear larger. The shillings looked like half-crowns and the sixpence like a shilling. I thought for a moment that it was because water magnifies, but I soon saw that this could not be the reason, for they went on growing larger, and of course thinner, until they finally spread into a kind of silver film all over the bottom of the pool; and as they did so the water began to take on a musical sound, much like the singing that comes when you wet your finger and draw it round the edge of a finger glass at dessert (which some people's idea of table manners allows them to do). It was a pretty sight and sound, and I listened and looked for a long time.

But all this time what had become of the plant ? Why, when I gave the silver to the spring I had wrapped the plant carefully in a silk handkerchief and put it safe in my breast pocket. I took the handkerchief out now, and for a moment I was afraid the plant was gone; but it was not. It had shrunk to a very small whity-green ball. Now what was to be done with it, or rather what could it do ? It was plain to me that it must have a strange and valuable property or virtue, since I had been put on its track in such a remarkable way. I thought I could not do better than ask the spring. I said, " O Spring of water, have I your good leave to ask what I should do with this precious plant to put it to the best use ? " The silver lining of the spring made its words much easier to catch when it said anything—for I should tell you that for the most part now it did not speak, or not in any language that I could under-stand, but rather sang—and it now said, " *Swallow swallow, drink, swallow.*"

Prompt obedience, dear Jane, has always been my motto, as it is doubtless yours, and I at once laid myself down, drank a mouthful of water from the spring, and put the little bulb in my mouth. It instantly grew soft and slipped down my throat. How prosaic! I have no idea what it tasted like.

And again I addressed the spring: "Is there anything more for me to do?"

"*No no, no no, you'll see, you'll see—good-bye, good-bye*," was the answer which came at once.

Accordingly I once more thanked the spring, wished it clear water, no mud, no tramplings of cattle, and bade it farewell. But, I said, I should hope to visit it again.

Then I turned away and looked about me, wondering whether, now that I had swallowed the mysterious plant, I should see anything different. The only thing I noticed was due, I suppose, not to the plant, but to the spring; but it was odd enough. All the trees hard by were crowded with little birds of all kinds sitting in rows on the branches as they do on telegraph wires. I have no doubt they were listening to the silver bell in the spring. They were quite still, and did not take any notice when I began to walk away.

I said, you will remember, that the ground I was on was a sort of flat terrace at the top of a steep slope. Now at one end this terrace just went down into the wood, but at the other end there was a little mound or hillock with thick underwood behind it. I felt a curiosity, an inclination, to walk that way: I have very little doubt that the plant was at the bottom of it. As I walked I looked at the ground, and noticed a curious thing: the roots of the plants and grasses seemed to show more than I was accustomed to see them.

It was not a great way to the hillock. When I got to it I wondered why I had gone, for there was nothing odd about it.

Still I stepped on to the top, and then I did see something, namely, a square flat stone just in front of my feet. I poked at it with my walking-stick, but somehow I did not seem to touch it, nor was there any scraping noise. This was funny. I tried again, and now I saw that my stick was not touching it at all; there was something in between. I felt with my hands, and they met with what seemed like grass and earth, certainly not like stone. *Then* I understood. The plant was the one which makes you able to see what is under the ground!

I need not tell you all I thought, or how surprising and delightful it was. The first thing was to get at the flat stone and find out what was underneath it.

Accordingly, what with a knife and what with my fingers, I soon had it uncovered : it was four or five inches under the surface. There were no marks on it; it measured more than a foot each way. I lifted it. It was the cover of a sort of box with bottom and sides each made of a slab just like the lid. In this box was another, made of some dark metal, which I took to be lead. I pulled it out and found that the lid of the box was all of one piece with the rest, like a sardine tin. Evidently I could not open it there and then. It was rather heavy, but I did not care, and I managed without too much inconvenience to carry it home to the place I was lodging in. Of course I put back the stone neatly and covered it up with earth and grass again.

I was late for tea, but I had found what was better than tea.

THE FIRST JAR

II

THE FIRST JAR

THAT night I waited till the moon was up before trying to open the box. I do not well know why, but it seemed the right thing, and I followed my instinct, feeling that it might be the plant that made me think as I did. I drew up the blind and laid the box on a table near the window, where the moon shone full on it, and waited to see if anything else occurred to me. Suddenly I heard a sort of metallic snap. I went and looked at the box. Nothing appeared on the side nearest to me—but when I turned it round I saw that all along the side which the moon had shone upon there was a line along the metal. I turned another side to the moonlight, and another snap came in two or three minutes. Of course I went on. When the moon had made a groove on all four sides, I tried the lid. It would not come off yet, so there was nothing to be done but continue the process. Three times I did it : every side I turned to the moon thrice, and when that was done the lid was free. I lifted it, and what did I see in the box ? All this writing would be very little use if I did not tell you, so it must be done.

There were five compartments in the box : in each of them was a little jar or vase of glass with a round body, a narrow neck, and spreading out a little at the top. The top of each was covered with a plate of metal and on each plate was a word or two in capital letters. On the one in the middle there were the words *unge oculos*, the other jars had one word apiece, *aures, linguam, frontem, pectus.*

Now, years ago, I took great pains to learn the Latin language, and on many occasions I have found it *most useful,* whatever you may see to the contrary in the newspaper : but seldom or never have I found it more useful than now. I saw at once that the words meant *anoint the eyes, the ears, the tongue, the forehead, the chest.* What would be the result of my doing this, of course I knew no more than you : but I was pretty sure that it would not do to try them all at once, and another thing I felt, that it would be better to wait till next day before trying any of them. It was past midnight now, so I went to bed : but first I locked up the box in a cupboard, for I did not want anyone to see it as yet.

Next day I woke bright and early, looked at my watch, found there was no need to think about getting up yet, and, like a wise creature, went to sleep again. I mention this, not merely by way of being jocose, but because after I went to sleep I had a dream which most likely came from

3

the plant and certainly had to do with the box.

I seemed to see a room, or to be in a room about which I only noticed that the floor was paved with mosaic in a pattern mostly red and white, that there were no pictures on the walls and no fireplace, no sashes or indeed panes in the window, and the moon was shining in very bright. There was a table and a chest. Then I saw an old man, rather badly shaved and bald, in a Roman dress, white for the most part, with a purple stripe somewhere, and sandals. He looked by no means a wicked or designing old man. I was glad of that. He opened the chest, took out my box, and placed it carefully on the table in the moonlight. Then he went to a part of the room I could not see, and I heard a sound of water being poured into a metal basin, and he came into sight again, wiping his hands on a white towel. He opened the box, took out a little silver spoon and one of the jars, took off

A FORMER OWNER OF THE JARS

the lid and dipped the spoon in the jar and touched first his right eye and then his left with it. Then he put the jar and the spoon back, laid the lid on the box and put it back in the chest. After that he went to the window and stood there looking out, and seemed to be very much amused with what he saw. That was all.

"Hints for me," I remember thinking. "Perhaps it will be best not to touch the box before the moon is up to-night, and always with washed hands." I suppose I woke up immediately, for it was all very fresh in my mind when I did.

It was something of a disappointment to have to put off my experiments till the night came round. But it was all for the best, for letters came by the post which I had to attend to: in fact, I was obliged to go to the town a little way off to see someone and to send telegrams and so on. I was a little doubtful about the seeing things underground, but I soon found that unless I—

so to say—turned on the tap, and specially wished and tried to use the power, it did not interfere with my ordinary seeing. When I did, it seemed to come forward from the back of my eyes, and was stronger than the day before. I could see rabbits in their burrows and followed the roots of one oak-tree very deep down. Once it threatened to be awkward, when I stooped to pick up a silver coin in the street, and grazed my knuckle against a paving stone, under which, of course, it was.

So much for that. By the way, I had taken a look at the box after breakfast, I found (not very much to my surprise) that the lid was as tight on it as when I found it first.

After dinner that evening I put out the light—the moon being now bright—placed the box on the table, washed my hands, opened it and, shutting my eyes, put my hand on one of the jars at random and took it out. As I had rather expected, I heard a little rattle as I did so, and feeling in the compartment, I found a little, a very little, spoon. All was well. Now to see which jar chance or the plant had chosen for my first experiment. I took it to the window : it was the one marked *aures*— ears—and the spoon had on the handle a letter **A**. I opened the jar. The lid fitted close but not over tightly. I put in the spoon as the old man had done, as near as I could remember. It brought out a very small drop of thick stuff with which I touched first my right ear and then my left. When I had done so I looked at the spoon. It was perfectly dry. I put it and the jar back, closed the box, locked it up, and, not knowing in the least what to expect, went to the open window and put my head out.

For some little time I heard nothing. That was to be expected, and I was not in the least inclined to distrust the jar. Then I was rewarded ; a bat flew by, and I, who have not heard a bat even squeak these twenty years, now heard this one say in a whistling angry tone, " Would you, would you, *I've* got you—no, drat, drat." It was not a very exciting remark, but it was enough to show me that a whole new world (as the books say) was open to me.

This, of course, was only a beginning. There were some plants and flowering shrubs under the window, and though I could see nothing, I began to hear voices—two voices—talking among them. They sounded young : of course they were anyhow very small, but they seemed to belong to young creatures of their kind.

" Hullo, I say, what have you got there ? Do let's look ; you might as well."

Then a pause—another voice : " I believe it's a bad one."

Number one : " Taste it."

Number two, after another pause, with a slight sound (very diminutive) of spitting : " Heugh ! bad ! I should rather think it was. Maggot ! "

Number one (after laughing rather longer than I thought kind): " Look here—don't chuck it away—let's give it to the old man. Here—shove the piece in again and rub it over—here he is ! " (Very demurely): " O sir, we've got such a nice-looking——" (*I could not catch what it was*) " here ; we thought you might perhaps like it, sir. Would you, sir ? . . . Oh no, thank you, sir, we've had plenty, sir, but this was the biggest we found."

A third voice said something ; it was a deeper one and less easy to hear.

Number two : " Bitten, sir ? Oh no, I don't think so. Do you —— ? " (*a name which I did not make out*).

Number one : " Why, how could it be ?

Number three again—angry, I thought.

Number two (rather anxiously): " But, sir, really, sir, I don't much like them. . . . Must I really, sir ? . . . O *sir*, it's got a maggot in it, and I believe they're poison." (*Smack, smack, smack, smack.*)

Two voices, very lamentable: "O *sir,* sir, please sir!"

A considerable pause, and sniffing. Then *Number two,* in a broken voice: "You silly fool, why did you go laughing like that right under his snout? You might have known he'd cog it." ("Cog." I had not heard the word since 1876.) "There'll be an awful row to-morrow. Look here, I shall go to bed."

The voices died away; I thought *Number one* seemed to be apologizing.

That was all I heard *that* night. After eleven o'clock things seemed to get very still, and I began to feel just a little apprehensive lest something of a less innocent kind should come along. So I went to bed.

THE SECOND JAR

III

THE SECOND JAR

NEXT day, I must say, was very amusing. I spent the whole of it in the fields just strolling about and sitting down, as the fancy took me, listening to what went on in the trees and hedges. I will not write down yet the kind of thing I heard, for it was only the beginning. I had not yet found out the way of using the new power to the very best advantage. I felt the want of being able to put in a remark or a question of my own every now and then. But I was pretty sure that the jar which had *linguam* on it would manage that.

Very nearly all the talking I heard was done by the birds and animals—especially the birds ; but perhaps half a dozen times, as I sat under a tree or walked along the road, I was aware of voices which sounded exactly like those of people (some grown-up and some children) passing by or coming towards me and talking to each other as they went along. Needless to say, there was nothing to be *seen* : no movement of the grass and no track on the dusty road, even when I could tell exactly where the people who owned the voices must be. It interested me more than anything else to guess what sort of creatures they were, and I determined that the next jar I tried should be the Eye one. Once, I must tell you, I ventured to say " Good afternoon " when I heard a couple of these voices within a yard of me. I think the owners must nearly have had a fit. They stopped dead : one of them gave a sort of cry of surprise, and then, I believe, they ran or flew away. I felt a little breath of wind on my face, and heard no more. It wasn't (as I know now) that they couldn't see me: but they felt much as you would if a tree or a cow were to say " Good afternoon " to you.

When I was at supper that evening, the cat came in, as she usually did, to see what was going. I had always been accustomed to think that cats talk when they mew, dogs when they bark, and so on. It is not so at all. Their talking is almost all done (except when they are in a great state of mind) in a tone which you cannot possibly hear without help. Mewing is for the most part only shouting without saying any words. Purring is, as we often say, singing.

Well, this cat was an ordinary nice creature, tabby, and in she came, and sat watching me while I had soup. To all appearance she was as innocent as a lamb —but no matter for that. What she was saying was something of this kind :

" Get on with it, do : shove it down, lap it up ! Who cares about soup ? Get to business. I know there's fish coming."

When the fish actually came, there was a great deal of good feeling shown at first. "Oh, *how* much we have to be thankful for, all of us, have we not? Fish, fish: what a thought! Dear, kind, generous people all around us, all striving to supply us with what is best and pleasantest for us."

Then there was a silence for a short time, then in a somewhat different tone I heard: "Ah dear! the longer I live, the wiser I find it is not to expect too much consideration from others! Self-love! how few, how terribly few, are really free from it! The nature that knows how to take a hint, how rare it is!"

Another short silence, and then: "There you go—another great bit. I wonder you don't choke or burst! Disgusting! A good scratch all down your horrible fat cheek is what you want, and I know some cats that would give it you. No more notion how to behave than a cockroach."

About this time I rang the bell and the

fish was taken away. The cat went too, circling round the maid with trusting and childlike glances, and I heard her saying in the former tone :

" Well, I daresay after all there are *some* kind hearts in the world, some that can feel for a poor weary creature, and know what a deal of strength and nourishment even the least bit of fish can give——" And I lost the rest.

When the time came and the box was open once more, I duly anointed my eyes and went to the window. I knew something of what I might expect to see, but I had not realized at all how much of it there would be. In the first place there were a great many buildings, in fact a regular village, all about the little lawn on which my window looked. They were, of course, not big; perhaps three feet high was the largest size. The roofs seemed to be of tiles, the walls were white, the windows were brightly lighted, and I could see people moving about inside. But there were plenty of people outside, too—people about six inches high—walking about, standing about, talking, running, playing some game which might have been hockey. These were on levelled spaces, for the grass, neatly kept as it was, would have come half-way up their legs; and there were some driving along smooth tracks in carriages drawn by horses of the right size, which were really the most charming little animals I ever saw.

You may suppose that I should not soon have got tired of watching them and listening to the little treble buzz of voices that went on, but I was interrupted. Just in front of me I heard what I can only call a snigger. I looked down, and saw four heads supported by four pairs of elbows leaning on the window-sill and looking up at me. They belonged to four boys who were standing on the twigs of a bush that grew up against the wall, and who seemed to be very much amused. Every now and again one of them nudged another and pointed towards me; and then, for some unexplained reason, they sniggered again. I felt my ears growing warm and red.

" Well, young gentlemen," I said, " you seem to be enjoying yourselves." No answer. " I appear to be so fortunate as to afford you some gratification," I went on, in my sarcastic manner. " Perhaps you would do me the honour of stepping into my poor apartment ? " Again no answer, but more undisguised amusement. I was thinking out a really withering remark, when one of them said :

" Do look at his nose. I wonder if they know how ridiculous they are. I *should* like to talk to one of them for five minutes."

" Well," I said, " that can be managed very easily, and I assure you I should be equally glad of the opportunity. *My* remarks would deal with the subject of good manners."

Another one spoke this time, but did not

4

answer me. "Oh, I don't know," he said, "I expect they're pretty stupid. They look it—at least this one does."

"Can they talk?" said the third. "I've never heard 'em."

"No, but you can see them moving their jaws and mouths and things. This one did just now."

I saw how it was now, and, becoming cooler, I recognized that these youths were behaving very much as I might have done myself in the presence of someone who I was sure could neither see nor hear me. I even smiled. One of them pointed at me at once:

"Thought of a joke, I s'pose. Don't keep it all to yourself, old chap."

At this moment the fourth, who had not said anything so far, but seemed to have been listening, piped up: "I say! I believe I know what it is that makes that hammering noise: it's something he has got in his clothes."

I could not resist this. "Right again," I said; "it's my watch, and you're very welcome to look at it." And I took it out and put it on the window-sill.

An awful horror and surprise came into their faces. In a second they had dived down like so many ducks. In another second I saw them walking across the grass, and each of them threw his arms round the waist or the neck of one of the elder people who were walking about among the houses. The person so attacked pulled himself up and listened attentively to what the boy was saying. The particular one I was watching looked towards my window and then burst out laughing, slapped the boy on the back, and resumed his walk. The boy went slowly off towards one of the houses. One or two of the other " men " came and stood nearer to the window, looking up. I thought I would venture a bow, and made one rather ceremoniously. It did not produce much effect, and I could not at the moment think of anything I could do that would show them quite clearly that I saw them. They went on looking at me quietly enough, and then I heard a deep low bell, seemingly very far off, toll five times. They heard it too, turned sharply round and walked off to the houses. Soon after that the lights in the windows died down and everything became very still. I looked at my watch. It was ten o'clock.

I waited for a while to see if anything would happen, but there was nothing; so I got some books out (which took a few minutes) and before I settled down to them I thought I would just take one more look out of the window. Where were all the little houses? At the first glance I thought they had vanished, but it was not exactly so. I found I could still see the chimneys above the grass, but as I looked they too disappeared. It was done very neatly: there was no hole, the turf closed in upon the roofs as they sank down, just as if it was of india-rubber. There was not a trace left of houses or roads or playgrounds or anything.

I was strongly tempted to go out and walk over the site of the village, but I did not. For one thing I was afraid I might disturb the people of the house, and besides there was a mist coming up over the meadows which sloped away outside the garden. So I stopped where I was.

But what a very odd mist, I began to think. It was not coming in all in one piece as it should. It was more in patches or even pillars of a smoky grey which moved at different rates, some of them occasionally standing still, others even seeming to go to and fro. And now I began to hear something like a hollow whispering coming from their direction. It was not conversation, for it went on quite continuously in the same tone: it sounded more as if something was being recited. I did not like it.

Then I saw what I liked less. Seven of

these pillars of mist, each about the size of a man, were standing in a row just outside the garden fence, and in each I thought I saw two dull red eyes ; and the hollow whispering grew louder.

Just then I heard a noise behind me in the room, as if the fire-irons had suddenly fallen down. So they had: and the reason why they had was that an old horseshoe which was on the mantelpiece had, for no reason that I could see, tumbled over and knocked them. Something I had heard came into my mind. I took the horseshoe and laid it on the window-sill. The pillars of mist swayed and quivered as if a sudden gust of wind had struck them, and seemed all at once to go farther off; and the hollow murmur was no longer to be heard. I shut the window and went to bed. But, the last thing, I looked out once again. The meadow was clear of mist and bright beneath the light of the moon.

As I lay in bed I thought and thought

THE PILLARS OF MIST

over what I had seen last. I was quite sure that the pillars of mist concealed some beings who wished me no good: but why should they have any spite against me ? I was also sure that they wanted to get into the house : but again, why ? You may think I was slow in the wits, but I must confess that some few minutes passed before I guessed. Of course they wanted to get hold of the box with the five jars. The thought disturbed me so much that I got up, lighted a candle, and went to the cupboard to see if all was safe. Yes, the box was there, but the cupboard door, which I knew I had locked, was unfastened, and when I had to turn the key it became plain that the lock was hampered and useless. How could this have come about ? Earlier in the evening it had been perfectly right, and nobody had been in the room since I locked it last.

Whoever had done it, they had made the cupboard no safe place for the box. I took it into the bedroom and after a minute's thought cleared out a space in a suit-case which I had brought with me, locked it in that, and put the key on the ring of my watch-chain. Watch and all went under my pillow, and once more I got into bed.

THE SMALL PEOPLE

IV

THE SMALL PEOPLE

YOU will have made sure that the next jar I meant to try was the one for the tongue, in hopes that it would help me to speak to some of the creatures. Though I looked forward to the experiment very much, and felt somewhat restless until I had made it, I did get a good deal of amusement out of what I saw and heard the next day. The small people were not to be seen—at least not in the morning. No, I am wrong: I found a bunch of three of them—young ones—asleep in a hollow tree. They woke up and looked at me without much interest, and when I was withdrawing my head they blew kisses to me. I am afraid there is no doubt they did so in derision. But there were others. I passed a cottage garden in which a little dog was barking most furiously. It seemed to be barking at a clothes-line, on which, with a lot of other things, was a print dress with rather a staring pattern of flowers. The dress caught my eye, and so did something red at the top which stuck up above the line. I gave it another glance, and really I had a most dreadful shock. It was a face. I gazed at it in horror, and was just gathering my wits to run and call for help or something, when I saw that it was laughing. Then I realized that it could not be an ordinary person, hanging as it was on a thin bit of cord and blowing to and fro in the breeze. I went nearer, staring at it with all my eyes, and made out that it was the face of an old woman, very cheerful and ruddy, and, as I said, laughing and swinging to and fro. Suddenly she seemed to catch my eye and to see that I saw her, and in a flash she was off the line and round the corner of the house, nearly tumbling over the dog as she went. It rushed after her, still very angry, but soon came trotting back, rather out of breath, and *that* incident was over.

I walked on. Among the village people I met, there were one or two whom I didn't think I had seen before—elderly, bright-eyed people they were—who seemed very much surprised when I said "Good morning" to them, and stopped still, looking after me, when I passed on. At last, some little way outside the village, I saw in the distance the same bright-coloured dress that had been on the clothes-line. The person who wore it was going slowly, and looking in the grass and hedges, and sometimes stooping to pick a plant, as it seemed. I quickened my pace and came up with her, and when I was just behind her, I cleared my throat rather loudly and said, "Fine day," or words to that effect.

You should have seen her jump! I was

well paid for the fright she had given me just before. However, the startled look cleared away from her face, and she drew herself up and looked at me very calmly.

"Yes," she said, "it's a fine day." Then she actually blushed and went on: "I think I ought to beg your pardon for giving you such a turn just now."

"Well," I said, "I certainly was a good deal startled, but no harm was done. The dog took it more to heart than I did."

She gave a short laugh. "Yes," she said. "I hardly know why I was behaving like that. I suppose we all of us feel skittish at times." She paused and said with some little hesitation, "You have them, I suppose?" and at the same time she rapidly touched her ears, eyes and mouth with her forefinger.

I looked at her in some doubt, for I thought, might not she be one of the unknown who wished to get hold of the Five Jars? But her eye was honest, and my instinct was to trust her : so I nodded, and put my finger on my lips.

" Of course," she said. " Well, you are the first since I was a little thing, and that's fourteen hundred years ago." (You may think I opened my eyes.) " Yes, Vitalis was the last, and he lived in the villa—they called it so—down by the stream. You'll find the place some of these days if you look. I heard talk yesterday that someone had got them, and I'm told the mist was about last night. Perhaps you saw it ? "

" Yes," I said, " I did, and I guessed what it meant." And I told her all that had happened, and ended by asking if she could kindly advise me what to do.

She thought for a moment, and then handed me a little bunch of the leaves she held in her hand. " Four-leaved clover," she said. " I know nothing better. Lay it on the box itself. You'll hear of them again, be sure."

" Who are *they* ? " I asked in a whisper.

She shook her head. " Not allowed," was all she would say. " I must be going " ; and she was gone, sure enough. You might suppose (as I did, when I came to think of it) that my new sight ought to have been able to see what became of her. I think it would, if she had gone straight away from me ; but what I believe she did was to dart round behind me and then go away in a straight line, so that I was left looking in front of me while she was travelling away behind me like a bullet from a gun. You need practice with these things, and I had only been at it a couple of days.

I turned and walked rather quickly homewards, for I thought it would be wise to protect my box as soon as possible now that I had the means. I think it was fortunate that I did.

As I opened the garden gate I saw an old woman coming down the path—an old woman very unlike the last. " Old " was not the word for her face: she might have been born before the history-books begin. As to her expression, if ever you saw a snake with red rims to its eyes and the expression of a parrot, you might have some idea of it. She was hobbling along with a stick, in quite the proper manner, but I felt certain that all that was put on, and that she could have glided as swift as an adder if she pleased. I confess I was afraid of her. I had a feeling that she knew everything and hated everybody.

" And what," I suddenly thought," has she been up to ? If she has got at the box, where am I ? and more than that, what mischief will she and her company work among the small people and the birds and beasts ? " There would be no mercy for them; a glance at her eye told me that.

It was an immense relief to see that she could not possibly have got the box about her, and another relief when my eye travelled to the door of the house and I

5

saw no fewer than three horseshoes nailed above it. I smiled to myself. Oh, how angry she looked! But she had to act her part, and with feeble curtseys and in a very small hoarse trembling voice she wished me a good day (though I noticed her pointing to the ground with her thumb as she said the words) and would be very obliged if I could tell her the right time. I was going to pull out my watch (and if I had, she would have seen a certain key we know of), when something said suddenly and clearly to my brain, "Look out," and by good luck I heard a clock inside the house strike one before I could answer.

"Just struck one," was my reply accordingly, and I said it as innocently as I could. She drew her breath in hard and quivered all over, and her mouth remained open like a cat's when it is using its worst expressions, and when she eventually thanked me I leave it to you to imagine how gracefully she did it.

Well, she had no more cards to play at the moment, and no excuse for remaining. I stood my ground and watched her out of the gate. A path led down the meadow, and, much against her will no doubt, she had to keep up the pretence and toil painfully along it until she reached another hedge and could reckon on being out of my sight. After that I neither saw nor expected to see anything more of her. I went up to my room and found all safe, and laid the four-leaved clover on the box. At luncheon I took occasion to find out from the maid, without asking her in so many words, whether the old woman had been visible to her ; evidently she had not : evidently also, the evil creatures were really on the track of the Five Jars, knew that I had them, and had a very fair idea of where they were kept.

However, if the maid had not seen her, the cat had, and murmured a good deal to herself, and was in a rather nervous state.

She sat, with her ears turned different ways, on the window-sill, looking out, and twitching her back uncomfortably, like an old lady who feels a draught. When I was available, she came and sat on my knee (a very uncommon attention on her part) with an air half of wishing to be protected and half of undertaking to protect me.

"If there is fish to-night," I said, "you shall have some." But I was not yet in a position to make myself understood.

"Pussy's been sleepin' on your box all the afternoon, sir," said the maid when I came in to tea. "I couldn't get her to come off; and when I did turn her out of the room, I do believe she climbed up and got in again by the winder."

"I don't mind at all," I said; "let her be there if she likes." And indeed I felt quite grateful to the cat. I don't know that she could have done much if there had been any attempt on the box, but I was sure her intentions were good.

There was fish that evening, and she had a good deal of it. She did not say much that I could follow, but chiefly sang songs without words.

*   *   *   *   *

Not to go over the preliminaries again, I did, when the proper time came, touch my tongue with the contents of the third jar. I found that it worked in this way: I could not hear what I was saying myself, when I was talking to an animal: I only *thought* the remark very clearly, and then I felt my tongue and lips moving in an odd fashion, which I can't describe. But with the small people in human shape it was different. I spoke in the ordinary way to them, and though I dare say my voice went up an octave or two, I can't say I perceived it.

The village was there again to-night, and the life going on in it seemed much the same. I was set upon making acquaintance in a natural sort of way with the people, and as it would not do to run any risk of startling them, I just took my place near the window and made some pretence of playing Patience. I thought it likely that some of the young people would come and watch me, in spite of the fright they had had the night before. And it was not long before I heard a rustling in the shrubs under the window and voices saying :

" Is he in there ? Can you see ? Oh, I say, *do* look out : you all but had me over that time ! "

They were suddenly quiet after this, and apparently one must have, very cautiously, climbed up and looked into the room. When he got down again there was a great fuss.

" No, is he really ? " " What d'you say he was doing ? " " What sort of charm ? " " I say, d'you think we'd better get down ? " " No, but what is he really doing ? " " Laying out rows of flat things on the table, with marks on them." " I

LIFE GOING ON MUCH AS USUAL

don't believe it." " Well, you go and look yourself." " All right, I shall." " Yes, but, I say, do look out: suppose you get shut in and we're late for the bell?" " Why, you fool, I shan't go into the room, only stop on the window-sill." " Well, I don't know, but I do believe he saw us last night, and my father said he thought so too." " Oh, well, he can't move very quick, anyway, and he's some way off the window. *I* shall go up."

I managed, without altering my position too much, to keep my eye on the window-sill, and, sure enough, in a second or two a small round head came into sight. I went on with my game. At first I could see that the watcher was ready to duck down at the slightest provocation, but as I took no sort of notice, he gained confidence, leant his elbows on the sill, and then actually pulled himself up and sat down on it. He bent over and whispered to the others below, and it was not long before I saw a whole row of heads filling up the window-sill from end to end. There must have been a dozen of them. I thought the time was come, and without moving, and in as careless a tone as I could, I said :

" Come in, gentlemen, come in; don't be shy." There was a rustle, and two or three heads disappeared, but nobody said anything. "Come in, if you like," I said again; " you can hear the bell quite well from here, and I shan't shut the window."

" Promise ! " said the one who was sitting on the sill.

" I promise, honour bright," I said, whereupon he made the plunge. First he dropped on to the seat of a chair by the window, and from that to the floor. Then he wandered about the room, keeping at a distance from me at first, and, I have no doubt, watching very anxiously to see whether I had any intention of pouncing on him. The others followed, first one by one and then two or three at a time. Some remained sitting on the window-sill, but most plucked up courage to get down on to the floor and explore.

I had now my first good chance of seeing what they were like. They all wore the same fashion of clothes—a tunic and close-fitting hose and flat caps—seemingly very much what a boy would have worn in Queen Elizabeth's time. The colours were sober—dark blue, dark red, grey, brown— and each one's clothes were of one colour all through. They had some white linen underneath; it showed a little at the neck. There were both fair and dark among them : all were clean and passably good-looking, one or two certainly handsome. The first-comer was ruddy and auburn-haired and evidently a leader. They called him Wag.

I heard whispers from corners of the room, and appeals to Wag to explain what this and that unfamiliar object was, and noticed that he was never at a loss for an answer of some kind, correct or not. The fireplace, which had its summer dressing, was, it appeared, a rock garden; an old letter lying on the floor was a charm (" Better not touch it "); the waste-paper basket (not unnaturally) a prison; the pattern on the carpet was—" Oh, you wouldn't understand it if I was to tell you."

Soon a voice—Wag's voice—came from somewhere near my foot.

" I say, could I get up on the top ? " I offered to lift him, but he declined rather hastily and said my leg would be all right if I didn't mind putting it out a bit sloping: and he then ran up it on all fours—he was quite a perceptible weight—and got on to the table from my knee without any difficulty.

Once there, there was a great deal to interest him—books, papers, ink, pens, pipes, matches and cards. He was full of questions about them, and his being so much at his ease encouraged the others to follow him, so that before very long the whole lot were perambulating the table and making me very nervous lest they should fall off, while Wag was standing close up to me and putting me through a catechism.

"What do you have such *little* spears for?" he wanted to know, brandishing a pen at me. "Is that blood on the end? whose blood? Well then, what do you do with it? Let's see—only that?" (when I wrote a word or two). "Well, you can tell me about it another time. Now I want to know what these clubs in the chest are."

I said, "We make fire with them; if you like I'll show you—but it makes a little noise."

"Go on," said Wag; and I struck a match, rather expecting a stampede. But no, they were quite unmoved, and Wag said, "Beastly row and smell—why don't you do the ordinary way?"

He brushed the palm of his left hand along the tips of the fingers on his right hand, put them to his lips and then to his eyes, and behold! his eyes began to glow from behind with a light which would have been quite bright enough for him to read by. "Quite simple," he said; "don't you know it?" Then he did the same thing in reverse order, touching eyes, lips and hand, and the light was gone. I didn't like to confess that this was beyond me.

"Yes, that's all very well," I said, "but how do you manage about your houses? I am sure I saw lights in the windows."

"Course," he said, "put as many as you want;" and he ran round the table dabbing his hand here and there on the cloth, or on anything that lay on it, and at every place a little round bud or drop of very bright but also soft light came out. "See?" he said, and darted round again, passing his hands over the lights and touching his lips; and they were gone. He came back and said, "It's a *much* better way; it is *really*," as if it were only my native stupidity that prevented me from using it myself.

A smaller one, who looked to me rather a quieter sort than Wag, had come up and was standing by him : he now said in a low voice :

" P'raps they can't."

It seemed a new idea to Wag : he made his eyes very round. " Can't ? Oh, rot ! it's quite simple."

The other shook his head and pointed to my hand which rested on the table. Wag looked at it too, and then at my face.

" Could I see it spread out ? " he said.

" Yes, if you'll promise not to spoil it."

He laughed slightly, and then both he and the other—whom he called Slim—bent over and looked closely at the tips of my fingers. " Other side, please," he said after a time, and they subjected my nails to a like examination. The others, who had been at the remoter parts of the table, wandered up and looked over their shoulders. After tapping my nails and lifting up one or more fingers, Wag stood upright and said :

"Well, I s'pose it's true, and you can't. I thought your sort could do anything."

"I thought much the same about you," I said in self-defence. "I always thought you could fly, but you——"

"So we can," said Wag very sharply, and his face grew red.

"Oh," I said, "then why haven't you been doing it to-night?"

He kicked one foot with the other and looked quickly at Slim. The rest said nothing and edged away, humming to themselves.

"Well, we *can* fly perfectly well, only——"

"Only not to-night, I suppose," said I, rather unkindly.

"No, *not* to-night," said Wag; "and you needn't laugh, either—we'll soon show you."

"That *will* be nice," I said; "and when will you show me?"

"Let's see" (he turned to Slim), "two nights more, isn't it? All right then (to me), in two nights more you'll see."

Just then a moth which flew in caused a welcome diversion—for I could see that somehow I had touched on a sore subject, and that he was feeling awkward—and he first jumped at it and then ran after it. Slim lingered. I raised my eyebrows and pointed at Wag. Slim nodded.

"The fact is," he said in a low voice, "he got us into rather a row yesterday and we're all stopped flying for three nights."

"Oh," said I. "I *see*: you must tell him I am very sorry for being so stupid. May I ask who stopped you?"

"Oh, just the old man, not the owls."

"You do go to the owls for something, then?" I asked, trying to appear intelligent.

"Yes, history and geography."

"To be sure," I said; "of course they've seen a lot, haven't they?"

"So they say," said Slim, "but——"

Just then the low toll of the bell was

wafted through the window and there was an instant scurry to the edge of the table, then to the seat of the chair, and up to the window-sill; small arms waved caps at me, the shrubs rustled, and I was left alone.

DANGER TO THE JARS

V

DANGER TO THE JARS

NOW my ears and eyes and tongue had been dealt with, and what remained were the forehead and the chest. I could not guess what would come of treating these with the ointment, but I thought I would try the forehead first. There was still a day or two when the moon would be bright enough for the trial. I hoped that perhaps the effect of these two last jars might be to make me able to go on with my experiences—to keep in touch with the new people I had come across—during the time when she—the moon, I mean—was out of sight.

I had one anxiety. The precious box must be guarded from those who were after it. About this I had a conviction, that if

I could keep them off until I had used each of the five jars, the box and I would be safe. Why I felt sure of this I could not say, but my experience had led me to trust these beliefs that came into my head, and I meant to trust this one. It would be best, I thought, if I did not go far from the house—perhaps even if I did not leave it at all till the time of danger was past.

Several things happened in the course of the morning which confirmed me in my belief. I took up a position at the table by the window of my sitting-room. I had put the box in my suit-case, which I had locked, and I now laid it beside me where I could keep an eye upon it. The view from my window showed me, first, the garden of the cottage, with its lawn and little flower beds, its hedge and back gate, and beyond that a path leading down across a field. More fields, I knew, came after that one, and sloped pretty sharply down to a stream in the valley, which I could not see; but I could see the steep slope of fields, partly pasture, and then clothed with green woods towards the top. There were no other houses in sight : the road was behind me, passing the front of the cottage, and my bedroom looked out that way. I had some writing and reading to do, and I had not long finished breakfast before I settled down to it, and heard the maid " doing out " the bedroom as usual, accompanied every now and then by a slight mew from the cat, who (also as usual) was watching her at work. These mews meant nothing in particular, I may say; they were only intended to be met by an encouraging remark, such as " There you are, then, pussy," or " Don't get in my way, now," or " All in good time." Finally I heard " Come along then, and let's see what we've got for you downstairs," and the door was shut. I mention this because of what happened about a quarter of an hour later.

There was suddenly a fearful crash in the

bedroom, a fall, a breaking of glass and crockery and snapping of wood, and then, fainter, sobbings and moans of pain. I started up.

" Goodness ! " I thought, " she must have been dusting that heavy shelf high up on the wall with all the china on it, and the whole thing has given way. She must be badly hurt! But why doesn't her mistress come rushing upstairs ? and what was that rasping noise just beside me ? "

I looked at my suit-case, which lay on the table just inside the open window. Across the new smooth top of it there were three deep scratches running towards the window, which had not been there before. I moved it to the other side of me and sat down. There had been an attempt to decoy me out of the room, and it had failed. Certainly there would be more.

I waited; but everything was quiet in the house : no more noise from the bed-room and no one moving about, upstairs or downstairs ; nothing but the pump clanking in the scullery. I turned to my work again.

Half an hour must have gone by, and, though on the look-out, I was not fidgety. Then I was aware of a confused noise from the field outside.

"Help! help! Keep off, you brute! Help, you there!" as well as I could make out, again and again. Towards the far end of the field, which was a pretty large one, a poor old man was trying to get to a gate in the hedge at a staggering run, and striking now and then with his stick at a great deer-hound which was leaping up at him with hollow barks. It seemed as if nothing but the promptest dash to the spot could save him; it seemed, too, as if he had caught sight of me at the window, for he beckoned. How strange the cries sounded! It was as if someone was shouting into an empty jug. My field-glasses were by me on the table, and I thought I would take just *one* look before I rushed out. I am glad

I did; for, do you know, when I had the glasses focused on the dog and the man, all that I could see was a sort of fuzz of dancing vapour, much as if the shimmering air that you see on the heath on a hot day had been gathered up and rolled into a shape.

"Ha! ha!" I said, as I put down the glasses; and something in the air, about four yards off, made a sharp hissing sound. No doubt there were words, but I could not distinguish them. A second attempt had failed; you may be sure I was well on the alert for the next.

I put away my books now, and sat looking out of the window, and wondering as I watched whether there was anything out of the common to be noticed. For one thing, I thought there were more little birds about than I expected. At first I did not see them, for they were not hopping about on the lawn; but as I stared at the hedge of the garden, and at that of the field, I became aware that these were full of life. On almost every twig that could hold a bird in shelter—not on the top of the hedges— a bird was sitting, quite still, and they were all looking towards the window, as if they were expecting something to happen there. Occasionally one would flutter its wings a little and turn its head towards its neighbour; but this was all they did.

I picked up my glasses and began to study the bottom of the hedges and the bushes, where there was some quantity of dead leaves, and here, too, I could see that there were spectators. A small bright eye or a bit of a nose was visible almost wherever I looked; in short, the mice, and, I don't doubt, some of the rats, hedgehogs, and toads as well, were collected there and were as intently on the watch as the birds. "What a chance for the cat, if only she knew!" I put my head cautiously out of the window, and looking down on the sill of the window below, I could see her head, with the ears pushed forward; she was looking earnestly at the hedge, but she did not move. Only, at the slight noise I made, she turned her face upwards and crowed to me in a modest but encouraging manner.

Time passed on. Luncheon was laid—on another table—and was over, before anything else happened.

The next thing was that I heard the maid saying sharply :

" What business 'ave you got going round to the back ? We don't want none of your rubbish here."

A hoarse voice answered inaudibly.

Maid : " No, nor the gentleman don't want none of your stuff neither; and how do you know there's a gentleman here at all I should like to know ? What ? Don't mean no offence ? I dare say. That's more than I know. Well, that's the last word I've got to say."

In a minute more there was a knock at my door, and at the same time a step on the gravel path under my window, and a loud hiss from the cat. As I said " Come in " to the knock, I hastily looked out of the window, but saw nothing. It was the maid who had knocked. She had come to ask if there was anything I should like from the village, or anything I should want before tea-time, because the mistress was going out, and wanted her to go over and fetch something from the shop. I said there was nothing except the letters and perhaps a small parcel from the post office. She lingered a moment before going, and finally said :

" You'll excuse me naming it, sir, but there seems to be some funny people about the roads to-day, if you'd please to be what I mean to say a bit on the look-out, if you're not a-going out yourself."

" Certainly," I said. " No, I don't mean to go out. By the way, who was it came to the door just now ? "

" Oh, it was one of these 'awking men, not one I've seen before, and he must be a stranger in this part, I think, because he began going round to the garden door, only I stopped him. He'd got these cheap rubbishing 'atpins and what not; leastways, if you understand me, what I thought to myself I shouldn't like to be seen with 'em, whatever others might."

"Yes, I see," I answered; and she went, and I turned to my books once more.

Within a very few minutes I began to suspect that I was getting sleepy. Yes, it was undoubtedly so. What with the warmth of the day, and lunch, and not having been out. . . . There was a curious smell in the room, too, not exactly nasty, like something burning. What did it remind me of? Wood smoke from a cottage fire, that one smells on an autumn evening as one comes bicycling down the hill into a village? Not quite so nice as that; something more like a chemist's shop. I wondered: and as I wondered, my eyes closed and my head went forward.

A sharp pain on the back of my hand, and a crash of glass! Up I jumped, and which of three or four things I realized first I don't know now. But I did realize in a second or two that my hand was bleeding from a scratch all down the back of it, that a pane of the window was broken and that the whole window was darkened with little birds that were bumping their chests against it; that the cat was on the table gazing into my face with intense expression, that a little smoke was drifting into the room, and that my suit-case was on the point of slipping out over the window-sill. A despairing dash at it I made, and managed to clutch it; but for the life of me I could not pull it back. I could see no string or cord, much less any hand that was dragging at it. I hardly dared to take my hand from it to catch up something and hack at the thief I could not see. Besides, there was nothing within reach.

Then I remembered the knife in my

pocket. Could I get it out and open it without losing hold? "They hate steel," I thought. Somehow—frantically holding on with one hand—I got out the knife, and opened it, goodness knows how, for it was horribly small and stiff, with my teeth, and sheared and stabbed indiscriminately all round the farther end of the suit-case. Thank goodness, the strain relaxed. I got the thing inside the window, dropped it, and stood on it, craning over the garden path and round the corner of the house. Of course there was nothing to be seen. The birds were gone. The cat was still on the table saying "O you owl! O you owl!" The sole and only clue to what had been happening was a small earthenware saucer that lay on the path immediately below the window, with a little heap of ashes in it, from which a thin column of smoke was coming straight up and curling over when it reached the window level. That, I could not doubt, was the cause of

THE CAT TAKES ACTION

my sudden sleepiness. I dropped a large book straight on to it, and had the satisfaction of hearing it crush to bits and of seeing the smoke go four ways along the ground and vanish.

I was perfectly awake now. I looked at the cat, and showed her the back of my hand. She sat quite still and said :

"Well, what did you expect? I had to do something. I'll lick it if you like, but I'd rather not. No particular ill-feeling, you understand ; all the same a hundred years hence."

I was not in a position to answer her, so I shook my head at her, wound up my hand in a handkerchief, and then stroked her. She took it agreeably, jumped off the table, and requested to be let out.

So the third attack had failed. I sat down and looked out. The hedges were empty ; not a bird, not a mouse was left. I took this to mean that the dangerous time was past, and great was the relief.

Soon I heard the maid come back from her errands in the village, then the mistress's chaise, then the clock striking five. I felt it would be all right for me to go out after tea.

And so I did; first, however, concealing the suit-case in my bedroom—not that I supposed hiding it would be of much use—and piling upon it poker, tongs, knife, horse-shoe, and anything else I could find which I thought would keep off trespassers. I had, by the way, to explain to the maid that a bird had flown against the window and broken it, and when she said "Stupid, tiresome little things they are," I am afraid I did not contradict her.

I went out by way of the garden and crossed the field, near the middle of which stands a large old oak. I went up to this, for no particular reason, and stood gazing at the trunk. As I did so I became aware that my eyes were beginning to "see through," and behold! a family of owls was inside.

As it was near evening, they were getting wakeful, stirring, smacking their beaks and opening their wings a little from time to time. At last one of them said :

" Time's nearly up. Out and about ! Out and about ! "

" Anyone outside ? " said another.

" No harm there," said the first.

This short way of talking, I believe, was due to the owls not being properly awake and consequently sulky. As they brightened up and got their eyes open, they began to be more easy in manner.

" Oop ! Oop ! Oop ! I've had a very good day of it. You have, too, I hope ? "

" Sound as a rock, I thank you, except when they were carrying on at the cottage."

" Oh goodness ! I forgot ! They didn't bring it off, I hope."

" Not they ; the watch was too well set, but it was wanted. I had a leaf about it a few minutes after, and it seems they got him asleep."

7

"Well! I never heard anyone bring a leaf."

"I dare say not, but I was expecting it; pigeon dropped it. There it is, on that child's back."

I saw the hen-owl stoop and examine a dead chestnut leaf which lay, as the other had said, on an owlet's back.

"Fa-a-ther!" said this owlet suddenly, in a shrill voice, "mayn't I go out to-night?"

But all that Father did was to clasp its head in his claw and push it to and fro several times. When he let go, the owlet made no sound, but crept away and hid its face in a corner, and heaved as if with sobs. Father closed his eyes slowly and opened them slowly—amused, I thought. The mother had been reading the leaf all the time.

"Dear me! *very* interesting!" she said. "I suppose now the worst of it is over."

"All's quiet for to-night, anyhow," said

THE OWL FAMILY

Father, " but I wish he could see someone about to-morrow; that's their last chance, and they *may*——" He ruffled up his feathers, lifted first one foot and then the other. " The awkwardness is," he went on, " if I say too much and they do get the jars, there's one risk; and if there's no warning and they get them, there's another risk."

" But if there *is* a warning and they *don't* get them," said she, very sensibly.

" Well, to be sure, that would be better, even though we don't know much about him."

" But where do you suppose he is, and whom ought he to see ? " (It was just what I wanted to know, and I thanked her.)

" Why, as to the first, I suspect he's outside; there is someone there, and why they should stop there all this time unless they're listening, I don't know."

" Good gracious ! listening to our private conversation ! and me with my feathers all anyhow ! " She began to peck at herself vigorously; but this was straying from the point, and annoyed me. However, Father went slowly on:

"As to that, I don't much care whether he's listening or not. As to whom he ought to see, that's rather more difficult. If he's got as far as talking to any of the Right People (he said this as if they had capital letters), they'd know, of course; and some of them down about the village, they'd know; and the Old Mother knows, and——"

"What about the boys?" said she, pausing in the middle of her toilet and poking her head up at him. He wholly disdained to answer, and merely butted at her with his head, so that she slipped down off her ledge several inches, with a great scrabbling. "Oh, *don't*!" she said peevishly, as she climbed back. "I'm all untidy again."

"Well then, don't ask such ridiculous questions. I shall buffle you with both wings next time. And now, as soon as the coast is clear, I shall be out and about."

I took the hint and moved off, for I had learnt as much perhaps as I could expect, even if all was not yet plain ; and before I had gone many paces I was aware of the pair both sailing smoothly off in the opposite direction.

I was " seeing through " a good deal that evening ; it is surprising what a lot of coppers people drop, even on a field path ; surprising, too, in how many places there lie, unsuspected, bones of men. Some things I saw which were ugly and sad, like that, but more that were amusing and even exciting. There is one spot I could show where four gold cups stand round what was once a book, but the book is no more than earth now. That, however, I did not see on this particular evening.

What I remember best is a family of young rabbits huddled round their parents in a burrow, and the mother telling a story : " And so then he went a little farther and found a dandelion, and stopped and sat up and began to eat it. And when he had eaten two large leaves and one little one, he saw a fly on it—no, two flies; and then he thought he had had enough of that dandelion, and he went a little farther and found another dandelion. . . ." And so it went on interminably, and entirely stupid, like everything else I ever heard a rabbit say, for they have forgotten all about their ancestor, Brer Rabbit. However, the children were absorbed in the story, so much so that they never heard a stoat making its way down the burrow. But I heard it, and by stamping and driving my stick in I was able to make it turn tail and go off, cursing. All stoats, weasels, ferrets, polecats, are of the wrong people, as you may imagine, and so are most rats and bats.

At last I left off seeing through, by trying not to do so, and went back to the house, where I found all safe and quiet.

I ought to say that I had not as yet tried speaking to any animal, even to the cat when she scratched me, but I thought I would try it now. So when she came in at dinner-time and circled about, with what I may call pious aspirations about fish and other such things, I summoned up my courage and said (using my voice in the way I described, or rather did not describe, before) :

"I used to be told, 'If you are hungry, you can eat dry bread.'"

She was certainly horribly startled. At first I thought she would have dashed up the chimney or out of the window; but she recovered pretty quickly and sat down, still looking at me with intense surprise.

"I suppose I might have guessed," she said; "but dear! what a turn you did give me! I feel quite faint; and gracious! what a day it has been! When I found you dozing off like a great—— Well, no one wants to be rude, do they? but I can tell you I had more than half a mind to go at your face."

" I am glad you didn't," I said; " and really, you know, it wasn't my fault: it was that stuff they were burning on the path."

" I know that well enough," she said; " but to come back to the point, all this anxiety has made me as empty in myself as a clean saucer."

" Just what I was saying; if you are hungry, you can——"

" Say that again, say it just once more," she said, and her eyes grew narrow as she said it, " and I shall——"

" What shall you do ? " I asked, for she stopped suddenly.

She calmed herself. " Oh, you know how it is when one's been all excited-like and worked up ; we all say more than we mean. But that about dry bread ! Well, there ! I simply can't bear it. It's a wicked, cruel untruth, that's what it is; and besides, you *can't* be going to eat all the whole of what she's put down for you." Excitement was coming on again, and she ended with a loud ill-tempered mew.

Well, I gave her what she seemed to want, and shortly after, worn out doubtless with the fatigues of the day, she went to sleep on a chair, not even caring to follow the maid downstairs when things were cleared away.

THE CAT, WAG, SLIM AND OTHERS

VI

THE CAT, WAG, SLIM AND OTHERS

I GOT out my precious casket. I sat by the window and watched. The moon shone out, the lid of the box loosened in due course, and I touched my forehead with the ointment. But neither at once nor for some little time after did I notice any fresh power coming to me.

With the moon, up came also the little town, and no sooner were the doors of the houses level with the grass than the boys were out of them and running in some numbers towards my window; in fact, some slipped out of their own windows, not waiting for the doors to be available. Wag was the first. Slim, more sedate, came among the crowd that followed. These were still the only two who felt no hesitation about talking to me. The others were all fully occupied in exploring the room.

"To-morrow," I said (after some sort of how-do-you-do's had been exchanged), "you'll be flying all over the place, I suppose."

"Yes," said Wag, shortly. "But I want to know—I say, Slim, what was it we wanted first?"

"Wasn't there a message from your father?" said Slim.

"Oh, yes, of course. 'If they're about the house,' he said, 'give them horseshoes; if there's a bat-ball, squirt at it': he thinks there's a squirt in the tool-house—Oh, there's the cat; I must——" After delivering all this in one sentence, he rushed to the edge of the table and took a kind of header into the midst of the unfortunate animal, who, however, only moaned or crowed without waking, and turned partly over on her back.

Slim remained sitting on a book and gazing soberly at me.

"Well," I said, "it's very kind of Wag's father to send me a message, but I must say I can't make much of it."

Slim nodded. "So he said, and he said you'd see when the time came; of course I don't know, myself; I've never seen a bat-ball. Wag says he has, but you never know with Wag."

"Well, I must do the best I can, I suppose; but look here, Slim, I wish you could tell me one or two things. What *are* you? What do they call you?"

"They call me Slim: and the whole of us they call the Right People," said Slim; "but it's no good asking us much, because we don't know, and besides, it isn't good for us."

"How do you mean?"

"Why, you see, our job is to keep the little things right, and if we do more than that, or if we try to find out much more, then we burst."

" And is that the end of you ? "

" Oh, no ! " he said cheerfully, " but that's one of the things it's no good asking."

" And if you don't do your job, what then ? "

" Oh, then they get smaller and have no sense." (He said *they*, not *we*, I noticed.)

" I see. Well now, you go to school, don't you ? " He nodded. " What for ? Isn't that likely to be bad for you ? " (I hardly liked to say " make you burst.")

" No," he said; " you see, it's to learn our job. We have to be told what used to go on, so as we can put things right, or keep them right. And the owls, you see, they remember a long way back, but they don't know any more than we do about the swell things."

I was very shy about putting the next question I had in mind, but I felt I must. " Now do you know how old you are, or how long it takes you to grow up, or how—how long you go on when you *are* grown up ! "

He pressed his hands to his head, and I was dreadfully afraid for the moment that it might be swelling and would burst; but it was not so bad as that. After a few seconds he looked up and said:

"I think it's seven times seven moons since I went to school and seven times seven times seven moons before I grow up; and the rest is no good asking. But it's all right"; upon which he smiled.

And this, I may say, was the most part of what I ventured to ask any of them about themselves. But at other times I gathered that as long as they "did their job" nothing could injure them; and they were regularly measured—all of them—to see if they were getting smaller, and a careful record kept. But if anyone lost as much as a quarter of his height, he was doomed, and he crept off out of the settlement. Whether such a one ever came back I could not be sure; most of the failures (and they were not common) went and

8

lived in hollow trees or by brooks, and were happy enough, but in a feeble way, not remembering much, nor able to make anything; and it was supposed that very slowly they shrunk to the size of a pin's point, and probably to nothing. All the same, it was believed that they *could* recover. Many other things that *you* would have asked, I did not, being anxious to avoid giving trouble.

But this time, anyhow, I felt I had catechized Slim long enough, so I broke off and said:

"What can Wag be doing all this while?"

"There's no knowing," said Slim. "But he's very quiet for him; either he's doing something awful, or he's asleep."

"I saw him with the cat last," I said; "you might go and look at her."

He walked to the edge of the table, and said, "Why, he *is* asleep!" And so he was, with his head on the cat's chest, under her chin, which she had turned up; and she had put her front paws together over the top of his head. As for the others, I descried them sitting in a circle in a corner of the room, also very quiet. (I imagine they were a little afraid of doing much without Wag, and also of waking him.) But I could not make out what they were doing, so I asked Slim.

"Racing earwigs, I should think," he said, with something of contempt.

"Well, I hope they won't leave them about when they go. I don't like earwigs."

"Who does?" he said; "but they'll take them away all right; they're prize ones, some of them."

I went over and looked at the racing for a little. The course was neatly marked out with small lights sprouting out of the boards, and the circle was at the winning-post, the starters being at the other end, some six feet away. I watched one heat. The earwigs seemed to me neither very speedy nor very intelligent, and all except one were apt to stop in mid-course and engage in personal encounters with each other.

I was beginning to wonder how long this would go on, when Wag woke up. Like most of us, he was not willing to allow that he had been asleep.

"I thought I'd just lie down a bit," he said, "and then I didn't want to bustle your cat, so I stopped there. And now I want to know—Slim, I say, what was it you were asking me?"

"Me asking you? I don't know."

"Oh, yes, you do; what he was doing the other time before we came in."

"I didn't ask you that; you asked me."

"Well, it doesn't matter who asked." (Turning to me): "What *were* you doing?"

"I don't know," I said. "Was it these things I was using" (taking up a pack of cards), "or something like this?" (I held up a book.)

"Yes, that one. What were you doing with it? What's it for?"

" We call it reading a book," and I tried to explain what the idea was, and read out a few lines ; it happened to be *Pickwick*. They were absorbed. Slim said, half to himself, " Something like a glass," which I thought quite meaningless at the time. Then I showed them a picture in another book. That they made out very quickly.

" But when's it going to move on ? " said Slim.

" Never," I said. " Ours stop just like that always. Do yours move on ? "

" Of course they do ; look here." He lay down on the tablecloth and pressed his forehead on it, but evidently could make nothing of it. " It's all rough," he said. I gave him a sheet of paper. " That's better ; " and he lay down again in the same posture for a few seconds. Then he got up and began rubbing the paper all over with the palms of his hands. As he did so a coloured picture came out pretty quickly, and when it was finished he drew aside to let me see, and said, somewhat bashfully, " I don't think I've got it *quite* right, but I meant it for what happened the other evening." He had certainly not got it right as far as I was concerned. It was a view of the window of the house, seen from outside by moonlight, and there was a back view of a row of figures with their elbows on the sill. So far, so good ; but inside the open window was standing a figure which was plainly—much too plainly, I thought—meant for me ; far too short and fat, far too red-faced, and with an owlish expression which I am sure I never wear. This person was now seen to move his hand—a very poor hand, with only about three fingers—to his side, and pull, apparently, out of his body, a round object more or less like a watch (at any rate it was white on one side with black marks, and yellow on the other) and lay it down in front of him. At this the figures at the window-sill threw up their arms in all directions and fell or slid down like so many dolls. Then the picture began to get fainter, and disappeared from the paper. Slim looked at me expectantly.

"Well," I said, "it's very interesting to see how you do it, but is that the best likeness of me that you can make?"

"What's wrong with it?" said he. "Isn't it handsome enough or something?"

I heard Wag throw himself down on the table, and, looking at him, I saw that he had got both hands pressed over his mouth.

"May I ask what the joke is?" I said rather dryly (for it is surprising how touchy one can be over one's personal appearance, even at my time of life). He looked up for an instant at me, and then gasped and hid his face again. Slim went up to him and kicked him in the ribs.

"Where's your manners?" he said in a loud whisper. Wag rolled over and sat up, wiping his eyes.

"I'm very sorry," he said. "I'm sure I

don't know what I was laughing for." Slim whistled. "Well," said Wag, "what *was* I?"

"Him, of course, and you know perfectly well!"

"Oh, was I? Well, perhaps you'll tell me what there is to laugh at about him?" said Wag, rather basely, I thought; so, as Slim put his finger to his lip and looked unhappy, I interrupted.

"Get up a minute, Wag," I said. "I want to see something."

"What?" said he, jumping up at once.

"Stand back to back with Slim, if you don't mind. That's it. Dear me! I thought you were taller than that—you looked to me taller last night. My mistake, I dare say. All right, thanks." But there they stood, gazing at each other with horror, and I felt I had been trifling with a most serious subject, so I laughed and said, "Don't disturb yourselves. I was only chaffing you, Wag, because you seemed to be doing something of the kind to me."

Slim understood, and heaved a sigh of relief. Wag sat down on a book and looked reproachfully upon me. Neither said a word. I was very much ashamed, and begged their pardon as nicely as I knew how. Luckily Wag was soon convinced that I was not in earnest, and he recovered his spirits directly.

"All *right*," he said, nodding at me; "did I hear you say you didn't like earwigs? That's worth remembering, Slim."

This reduced me at once; I tried to point out that he had begun it, and that it would be a mean revenge, and very hard on the earwigs, if he filled my room with them, for I should be obliged to kill all I could.

"Why," he said, "they needn't be real earwigs; my own tickle every bit as much as real ones."

This was no better for me, and I tried to make more appeals to his better feelings.

He did not seem to be listening very attentively, though his eyes were fixed on me.

"What's that on your neck?" he said suddenly, and at the same moment I felt a procession of legs walking over my skin. I brushed at it hastily, and something seemed to fall on the table. "No, the other side I mean," said he, and again I felt the same horrid tickling and went through the same exercises, with a face, I've no doubt, contorted with terror. Anyhow, it seemed to amuse them very much; Wag, in fact, was quite unable to speak, and could only point. It was dull of me not to have realized at once that these were "his" earwigs and not real ones. But now I did, and though I still felt the tickling, I did not move, but sat down and gazed severely at him. Soon he got the better of his mirth and said, "I think we are quits now." Then, with sudden alarm, "I say, what's become of the others? The bell hasn't gone, has it?"

"How should I know?" I said. "If

you hadn't been making all this distur-
bance, perhaps we might have heard it."

He took a flying leap—an extraordinary
feat it was—from the edge of the table to
a chair in the window, scrambled up to
the sill, and gazed out. "It's all right,"
he said, in a faint voice of infinite relief;
let himself down limply to the floor, and
climbed slowly up my leg to his former
place.

"Well," I said, "the bell hasn't gone, it
seems, but where are the rest? I've hardly
seen anything of them."

"Oh, *you* go and find 'em, Slim; I'm
worn out with all these frights."

Slim went to the farther end of the
table, prospected, and returned. He re-
ported them "all right, but they're having
rather a slow time of it, I think." I, too,
got up, walked round, and looked; they
were seated in a solemn circle on the floor
round the cat, who was now curled up and
fast asleep on a round footstool. Not a

word was being said by anybody. I thought I had better address them, so I said :

" Gentlemen, I'm afraid I've been very inattentive to you this evening. Isn't there anything I can do to amuse you ? Won't you come up on the table ? You're welcome to walk up my leg if you find that convenient."

I was almost sorry I had spoken the moment after, for they made but one rush at my legs as I stood by the table, and the sensation was rather like that, I imagine, of a swarm of rats climbing up one's trousers. However, it was over in a few seconds, and all of them—over a dozen—were with Wag and Slim on the table, except one, who, whether by mistake or on purpose, went on climbing me by way of my waistcoat buttons, rather deliberately, until he reached my shoulder. I didn't object, of course, but I turned round (which made him catch at my ear) and went back to my chair, seated in which I felt rather as if I was presiding at a meeting. The one on my shoulder sat down and, I thought, folded his arms and looked at his friends with some triumph. Wag evidently took this to be a liberty.

"My word!" he said, "what do you mean by it, Wisp? Come off it!"

Wisp was a little daunted, as I judged by his fidgeting somewhat, but put a bold face on it and said, "Why should I come off?"

I put in a word: "I don't mind his being here."

"I dare say not; that's not the point," said Wag. "Are you coming down?"

"No," said Wisp, "not for you." But his tone was rather blustering than brave.

"Very well, don't then," said Wag; and I expected him to run up and pull Wisp down by the legs, but he didn't do that. He took something out of the breast of his tunic, put it in his mouth, lay down on his stomach, and, with his eyes on Wisp, puffed out his cheeks. Two or three seconds passed, during which I felt Wisp shifting about on his perch, and breathing quickly. Then he gave a sharp shriek, which went right through my head, slipped rapidly down my chest and legs and on to the floor, where he continued to squeal and to run about like a mad thing, to the great amusement of everyone on the table.

Then I saw what was the matter. All round his head were a multitude of little sparks, which flew about him like a swarm of bees, every now and then settling and coming off again, and, I suppose, burning him every time; if he beat them off, they attacked his hands, so he was in a bad way. After watching him for about a minute from the edge of the table, Wag called out:

"Do you apologize?"

"Yes!" he screamed.

"All right," said Wag; "stand still! stand still, you bat! How can I get 'em back if you don't?" Wag was back to me and I couldn't see what he did, but Wisp sat down on the carpet free of sparks, and wiped his face and neck with his handkerchief for some time, while the rest gradually recovered from their laughter. " You can come up again now," said Wag; and so he did, though he was slow and shy about it.

" Why didn't he send sparks at Wag ? " said I to Slim.

" He hasn't got 'em to send," was the answer. " It's only the Captain of the moon."

" Well now, what about a little peace and quiet ? " I said. " And, you know, I've never been introduced to you all properly. Wouldn't it be a good idea to do that, before the bell goes ? "

" Very well," said Wag. " We'll *do* it properly. You bring 'em up one at a time, Slim, and " (to me) " you put your sun-hand out on the table."

(*I :* " Sun-hand ? "

Wag : " Yes, sun-hand ; don't you

know ? " He held up his right hand, then his left : " Sun-hand, Moon-hand, Day-hand, Night-hand, Star-hand, Cloud-hand, and so on."

I : " Thank you.")

This was done, and meanwhile Slim formed the troop into a queue and beckoned them up one by one. Wag stood on a book on the right and proclaimed the name of each. First he had made me arrange my right hand edgeways on the table, with the forefinger out. Then " Gold ! " said Wag. Gold stepped forward and made a lovely bow, which I returned with an inclination of my head, then took as much of my forefinger top joint in his right hand as he could manage, bent over it and shook it or tried to, and then took up a position on the left and watched the next comer. The ceremony was the same for everyone, but not all the bows were equally elegant ; some of the boys were jocular, and shook my finger with both hands and a great

WAG INTRODUCES THE PARTY

display of effort. These were frowned upon by Wag. The names (I need not set them all down now) were all of the same kind as you have heard; there was Red, Wise, Dart, Sprat, and so on. After Wisp, who came last and was rather humble, Wag called out Slim, and, after him, descended and presented himself in the same form.

"And now," he said, "perhaps you'll tell us *your* name."

I did so (one is always a little shame-faced about it, I don't know why) in full. He whistled.

"Too much," he said; "what's the easiest you can do?"

After some thought I said, "What about M or N?"

"Much better! If M's all right for you, it'll do for us." So M was agreed upon.

I was still rather afraid that the rank and file had been passing a dull evening and would not come again, and I tried to express as much to them. But they said:

"Dull? Oh no, M; why we've found out all sorts of things!"

"Really? What sort of things?"

"Well, inside the wall in that corner there's the biggest spider I've ever seen, for one thing."

"Good gracious!" I said. "I hate 'em. I hope it can't get out?"

"It would have to-night if we hadn't stopped up the hole. Something's been helping it to gnaw through."

"Has it?" said Wag. "My word! that looks bad. What was it made the hole?"

Some called out, "A bat," and some "A rat."

"It doesn't matter much for that," said Slim, "so long as it's safe now. Where is it?"

"Gone down to the bottom and saying awful things," Red answered.

"Well, I *am* obliged to you," I said. "Anything else?"

"There's a lot of this stuff under the

floor," said Dart, pointing with his foot at a half-crown which lay on the table.

"Is there? Whereabouts?" said I. "Oh, but I was forgetting; I can look after that myself."

"Yes, of course you can," they said; "and lots of things happened here before you came. We were watching. The old man and the woman, they were the worst, weren't they, Red?"

"Do you mean you've been here before?" I asked.

"No, no, but to-night we were looking at them, like we do at school."

This was beyond me, and I thought it would be of no use to ask for more explanations. Besides, just at this moment we heard the bell. They all clambered down either me or the chairs or the tablecloth. Slim lingered a moment to say, "You'll look out, won't you?" and then followed the rest on to the window-sill, where, taking the time from Captain Wag, they all stood in a row, bowed with their caps off, straightened up again, each sang one note, which combined into a wonderful chord, faced round and disappeared. I followed them to the window and saw the inhabitants of the house separating and going to their homes with the young ones capering round them. One or two of the elders—Wag's father in particular—looked up at me, paused in their walk, and bowed gravely, which courtesy I returned. I went on gazing until the lawn was a blank once more, and then, closing and fastening the sitting-room window, I betook myself to the bedroom.

THE BAT-BALL

VII

THE BAT-BALL

IT had certainly been an eventful day and evening, and I felt that my adventures could not be quite at an end yet, for I had still to find out what new power or sense the Fourth Jar had brought me. I stood and thought, and tried quite vainly to detect some difference in myself. And then I went to the window and drew the curtain aside and looked out on the road, and within a few minutes I began to understand.

There came walking rapidly along the road a young man, and he turned in at the garden gate and came straight up the path to the house door. I began to be surprised, not at his coming, for it was not so very late, but at the look of him. He was young, as I said, rather red-faced, but not bad-looking; of the class of a farmer, I thought. He wore biggish brown whiskers —which is not common nowadays—and his hair was rather long at the back— which also is not common with young men who want to look smart—-but his hat, and his clothes generally, were the really odd part of him. The hat was a sort of low top-hat, with a curved brim; it spread out at the top and it was brushed rough instead of smooth. His coat was a blue swallow-tail with brass buttons. He had a broad tie wound round and round his neck, and a Gladstone collar. His trousers were tight all the way down and had straps under his feet. To put it in the dullest, shortest way, he was "dressed in the fashion of eighty or ninety years ago," as we read in the ghost stories. Evidently he knew his way about very well. He came straight up to the front door and, as far as I could tell, into the house, but I did not hear the door open or shut or any steps on the stairs. He must, I thought, be in my landlady's parlour downstairs.

I turned away from the window, and there was the next surprise. It was as if there was no wall between me and the sitting-room. I saw straight into it. There was a fire in the grate, and by it were sitting face to face an old man and an old woman. I thought at once of what one of the boys had said, and I looked curiously at them. They were, you would have said, as fine specimens of an old-fashioned yeoman and his wife as anyone could wish to see. The man was hale and red-faced, with grey whiskers, smiling as he sat bolt upright in his arm-chair. The old lady was rosy and smiling too, with a smart silk dress and a smart cap, and tidy ringlets on each side of her face—a regular picture of wholesome old age ; and yet I hated them both. The young man, their son, I suppose, was in the room standing at the door with his hat in his hand, looking timidly at them. The old man turned half round in his chair, looked at him, turned down the corners of his mouth, looked across at the old lady, and they both smiled as if they were amused. The son came farther into the room, put his hat down, leaned with both hands on the table, and began to speak (though nothing could be heard) with an earnestness that was painful to see, because I could be certain his pleading would be of no use; sometimes he spread out his hands and shook them, every now and again he brushed his eyes. He was very much moved, and so was I, merely watching him. The old people were not; they leaned forward a little in their chairs and sometimes smiled at each other—again as if they were amused. At last he had done, and stood with his hands before him, quivering all over. His father and mother leaned back in their chairs and looked at each other. I think they said not a single word.

The son caught up his hat, turned round, and went quickly out of the room. Then the old man threw back his head and laughed, and the old lady laughed too, not so boisterously.

I turned back to the window. It was as I expected. Outside the garden gate, in the road, a young slight girl in a large poke-bonnet and shawl and rather short-skirted dress was waiting, in great anxiety, as I could see by the way she held to the railings. Her face I could not see. The young man came out; she clasped her hands, he shook his head; they went off together slowly up the road, he with bowed shoulders, supporting her, she, I dare say, crying. Again I looked round to the sitting-room. The wall hid it now.

It sounds a dull ordinary scene enough, but I can assure you it was horribly disturbing to watch, and the cruel calm way in which the father and mother, who looked so nice and worthy and were so abominable, treated their son, was like nothing I had ever seen.

Of course I know now what the effect of the Fourth Jar was; it made me able to see what had happened in any place. I did not yet know how far back the memories would go, or whether I was obliged to see them if I did not want to. But it was clear to me that the boys were sometimes taught in this way. "We were watching them like we do at school," one of them said, and though the grammar was poor, the meaning was plain, and I would ask Slim about it when we next met. Meanwhile I must say I hoped the gift would not go on working instead of letting me go to sleep. It did not.

Next day I met my landlady employing herself in the garden, and asked her about the people who had formerly lived in the house.

"Oh yes," said she. "I can tell you about them, for my father he remembered old Mr. and Mrs. Eld quite well when he was a slip of a lad. They wasn't liked in the place, neither of them, partly through bein' so hard-like to their workpeople, and partly from them treating their only son so bad—I mean to say turning him right off because he married without asking permission. Well, no doubt, that's what he shouldn't have done, but my father said it was a very nice respectable young girl he married, and it do seem hard for them never to say a word of kindness all those years and leave every penny away from the young people. What become of them, do you say, sir? Why, I believe they emigrated away to the United States of America and never was heard of again, but the old people they lived on here, and I never heard but what they was easy in their minds right up to the day of their death. Nice-looking old people they was too, my father used to say; seemed as if butter wouldn't melt in their mouths, as the saying is. Now I don't know when I've thought of them last, but I recollect my father speaking of them as well as well, and the way they're spoke of on their stone that lays just to the right-hand side as you go up the churchyard path—well, you'd think there never was such people. But I believe that was put up by them that got the property; now what was that name again?"

But about that time I thought I must be getting on. I also thought (as before) that it would be well for me not to go very far away from the house.

As I strolled up the road I pondered over the message which Wag's father had been so good as to send me. "If they're about the house, give them horseshoes; if there's a bat-ball, squirt at it. I think there's a squirt in the tool-house." All very well, no doubt. I had one horseshoe, but that was not much, and I could explore the tool-house and borrow the garden squirt. But more horseshoes?

At that moment I heard a squeak and a rustle in the hedge, and could not help poking my stick into it to see what had made the noise. The stick clinked against something with its iron ferrule. An old horseshoe!—evidently shown to me on purpose by a friendly creature. I picked it up, and, not to make a long story of it, I was helped by much the same devices to increase my collection to four. And now I felt it would be wise to turn back.

As I turned into the back garden and came in sight of the little potting-shed or tool-house or whatever it was, I started. Someone was just coming out of it. I gave a loud cough. The party turned round hastily; it was an old man in a sleeved waistcoat, made up, I thought, to look like an " odd man." He touched his hat civilly enough, and showed no surprise; but, oh, horror! he held in his hand the garden squirt.

" Morning," I said; " going to do a bit

of watering ? " He grinned. " Just stepped up to borrer this off the lady; there's a lot of fly gets on the plants this weather."

" I dare say there is. By the way, what a lot of horseshoes you people leave about. How many do you think I picked up this morning just along the road ? Look here ! " and I held one out to him, and his hand came slowly out to meet it, as though he could not keep it back.

His face wrinkled up into a horrible scowl, and what he was going to say I don't know, but just then his hand clutched the horseshoe and he gave a shout of pain, dropped the squirt and the horseshoe, whipped round as quick as any young man could, and was off round the corner of the shed before I had really taken in what was happening. Before I tried to see what had become of him, I snatched up the squirt and the horseshoe, and almost dropped them again. Both were pretty hot—the squirt much the hotter of the two; but both of them cooled down in a few seconds. By that time my old man was completely out of sight. And I should not wonder if he was away some time; for perhaps you know, and perhaps you don't know, the effect of an old horseshoe on that sort of people. Not only is it of iron, which they can't abide, but when they see or, still more, touch the shoe, they have to go over all the ground that the shoe went over since it was last in the blacksmith's hands. Only I doubt if the same shoe will work for more than one witch or wizard. Anyway, I put that one aside when I went indoors. And then I sat and wondered what would come next, and how I could best prepare for it. It occurred to me that it would do no harm to put one of the shoes where it couldn't be seen at once, and it also struck me that under the rug just inside the bedroom door would not be a bad place. So there I put it, and then fell to smoking and reading.

10

A knock at the door.

"Come in," said I, a little curious; but no, it was only the maid. As she passed me (which she did quickly) I heard her mutter something about "'ankerchieves for the wash," and I thought there was something not quite usual about the voice. So I looked round. She was back to me, but the dress and the height and the hair was what I was accustomed to see. Into the bedroom she hurried, and the next thing was a scream like that of at least two cats in agony! I could just see her leap into the air, come down again on the rug, scream again, and then bundle, hopping, limping— I don't know what—out of the room and down the stairs. I did catch sight of her feet, though; they were bare, they were greenish, and they were webbed, and I think there were some large white blisters on the soles of them. You would have thought that the commotion would have brought the household about my ears; but it did not, and I can only suppose that they heard no more of it than they did of the things which the birds and so on say to each other.

"Next, please!" said I, as I lighted a pipe; but if you will believe it, there was no next. Lunch, the afternoon, tea, all passed by, and I was completely undisturbed. "They must be saving up for the bat-ball," I thought. "What in the world can it be?"

As candle-time came on, and the moon began to make herself felt, I took up my old position at the window, with the garden squirt at hand and two full jugs of water on the floor—plenty more to be got from the bathroom if wanted. The leaden box of the Five Jars was in the right place for the moonbeams to fall on it. . . . But no moonbeams would touch it to-night! Why was this? There were no clouds. Yet, between the orb of the moon and my box, there was some obstruction. High up in the sky was a dancing film, thick enough to cast a shadow on the area of the window; and ever, as the moon rode higher in the heavens, this obstruction became more solid. It seemed gradually to get its bearings and settle into the place where it would shut off the light from the box most completely. I began to guess. It was the bat-ball; neither more nor less than a dense cloud of bats, gradually forming itself into a solid ball, and coming lower, and nearer to my window. Soon they were only about thirty feet off, and I felt that the moment was come.

I have never much liked bats or desired their company, and now, as I studied them through the glass, and saw their horrid little wicked faces and winking wings, I felt justified in trying to make things as unpleasant for them as I could. I charged the squirt and let fly, and again, and again, as quick as I could fill it. The water spread a bit before it reached the ball, but not too much to spoil the effect; and the effect was almost alarming. Some hundreds of bats all shrieking out at once, and shrieking with rage and fear (not merely from the excitement of chasing flies, as they generally do). Dozens of them dropping away, with wings too soaked to fly, some on to the grass, where they hopped and fluttered and rolled in ecstasies of passion, some into bushes, one or two plumb on to the path, where they lay motionless; that was the first tableau. Then came a new feature. From both sides there darted into the heart of the ball two squadrons of figures flying at great speed (though without wings) and perfectly horizontal, with arms joined and straight out in front of them, and almost at the same instant seven or eight more plunged into the ball from above, as if taking headers. The boys were out.

I stopped squirting, for I did not know whether the water would fell them as it felled the bats ; but a shrill cry rose from below :

"Go on, M ! go on, M ! "

So I aimed again, and it was time, for a knot of bats just then detached itself from the main body and flew full-face towards me. My shot caught the middle one on the snout, and as I swung the squirt to left and right, it disabled four or five others, and discouraged the rest. Meanwhile the ball was cloven again and again by the arms of the flying squadrons, which shot through it from side to side and from top to bottom (though never, as appeared later, quite through the middle), and though it kept closing up again, it was plainly growing smaller as more and more of the bats outside, which were exposed to the squirt, dropped away.

I suddenly felt something alight on my shoulder, and a voice said in my ear, " Wag says if you *could* throw a shoe into the middle now, he believes it would finish them.

Can you?" It was, I think, Dart who had been sent with the message.

"Horseshoes, I suppose he means," I said. "I'll try."

"Wait till we're out of the way," said Dart, and was off.

In a moment more I heard—not what I was rather expecting, a horn of Elf-land, but two strokes on the bell. I saw the figures of the boys shoot up and away to left and right, leaving the bat-ball clear, and the bats shrieked aloud, I dare say in triumph at the enemy's retreat.

There were two horseshoes left. I had no idea how they would fly, and I had not much confidence in my power of aiming; but it must be tried, and I threw them edgeways, like quoits. The first skimmed the top of the ball, the second went straight through the middle. Something which the bats in the very centre were holding— something soft—was pierced by it, and burst. I think it must have been a globe of jelly-like stuff in a thin skin. The contents spurted out on to some of the bats, and seemed to scald the fur off them in an instant and singe up all the membranes of their wings. They fell down at once, with broken screams. The rest darted off in every direction, and the ball was gone.

"Now don't be long," said a voice from the window-sill.

I thought I knew what was meant, and looked to the leaden casket. As if to make up for lost time, the moonbeam had already made an opening all round the part on which it shone, and I had but to turn the other side towards it—not even very slowly —to get the whole lid free. After cleansing my hands in the water, I made trial of the Fifth Jar, and, as I replaced it, a chorus of applause and cheering came up from below.

The Jars were mine.

WAG AT HOME

VIII

WAG AT HOME

THERE was no scrambling up to the window-sill this time. My visitors shot in like so many arrows, and "brought up" on their hands on the tablecloth, or lit on their feet on the top rail of a chair-back or on my shoulder, as the fancy took them. It would be tedious to go through all the congratulations and thanks which I offered, and indeed received, for it was important to them that the Jars should not get into wrong hands.

"Father says," said Wag, who was sitting on a book, as usual—"Oh, what fun it is to be able to fly again!" And he darted straight and level and butted head first

155

into the back of—Sprat, was it ?—who was standing near the edge of the table. Sprat was merely propelled into the air a foot or two off, and remained standing, but, of course, turned round and told Wag what he thought of him. Wag returned contentedly to his book. "Father says," he resumed, "he hopes you'll come and see us now. He says you did all right, and he's very glad the stuff got spilt, because they'll take moons and moons to get as much of it together again. He says they meant to squirt some of it on you when they got near enough, and while you were trying to get it off they'd have got hold of——" He pointed to the box of jars; there was a shyness about mentioning it.

"Your father's very kind," I said, "and I hope you'll thank him from me; but I don't quite see how I'm to get into your house."

"Fancy you not knowing that !" said Wag. "I'll tell him you'll come." And he he was out of the window. As usual, I had recourse to Slim.

"Why, you did put some on your chest, didn't you?" was Slim's question.

"Yes, but nothing came of it."

"Well, I believe you can go pretty well anywhere with that, if you think you can."

"Can I fly, then?"

"No, I should say not; I mean, if you couldn't fly before, you can't now."

"How do you fly? I don't see any wings."

"No, we never have wings, and I'm rather glad we don't; the things that have them are always going wrong somehow. We just work it in the proper way with our backs, and there you are; like this." He made a slight movement of his shoulders, and was standing in the air an inch off the table. "You never tried that, I suppose?" he went on.

"No," I said, "only in dreams," which evidently meant nothing to him. "Well now," I said, "do you tell me that if I went to Wag's house now, I could get inside it? Look at the size I am!"

"It doesn't look as if you could," he agreed, "but my father said just the same as Wag's father about it."

Here Wag shot on to my shoulder. "Are you coming?"

"Yes, if I knew how."

"Well, come and try, anyhow."

"Very well, as you please; anything to oblige."

I picked up a hat and went downstairs. All the rest followed, if you can call it following, when there was at least as much flying up steps and in and out of banisters as going down. When we were out on the path, Wag said with more seriousness than usual:

"Now you do mean to come into our house, don't you?"

"Certainly I do, if you wish me to."

"Then that's all right. This way. There's Father."

We were on the grass now, and very long it was, and nice and wet I thought I should be with all the dew. As I looked up to see the elder Wag I very nearly fell over a large log which it was very careless of anyone to have left about. But here was Mr. Wag within a yard of me, and to my extreme surprise he was quite a size-able man of middle height, with a sensible, good-humoured face, in which I could see a strong likeness to his son. We both bowed, and then shook hands, and Mr. Wag was very complimentary and pleasant about the occurrences of the evening.

" We've pretty well got the mess cleared up, you see. Yes, don't be alarmed," he went on, and took hold of my elbow, for he had, no doubt, seen a bewildered look in my eyes. The fact was, as I suppose you have made out, not that he had grown to my size, but that I had come down to his. " Things right themselves ; you'll have no difficulty about getting back when the time comes. But come in, won't you ? "

You will expect me to describe the house and the furniture. I shall not, further than to say that it seemed to me to be of a piece with the fashion in which the boys were dressed; that is, it was like my idea of a good citizen's house in Queen Elizabeth's time; and I shall not describe Mrs. Wag's costume. She did not wear a ruff, anyhow.

Wag, who had been darting about in the air while we walked to his home, followed us in on foot. He now reached up to my shoulder. Slim, who came in too, was shorter.

"Haven't you got any sisters?" I took occasion to say to Wag.

"Of course," said he; "don't you see 'em? Oh! I forgot. Come out, you sillies!"

Upon which there came forward three nice little girls, each of whom was putting away something into a kind of locket which she wore round her neck. No, it is no use asking me what *their* dresses were like ; none at all. All I know is that they curt-sied to me very nicely, and that when we all sat down the youngest came and put herself on my knee as if it was a matter of course.

" Why didn't I see you before ? " I asked her.

" I suppose because the flowers were in our hair."

" Show him what you mean, my dear," said her father. " He doesn't know our ways yet."

Accordingly she opened her locket and took out of it a small blue flower, looking as if it was made of enamel, and stuck it in her hair over her forehead. As she did so she vanished, but I could still feel the weight of her on my knee. When she took it out again (as no doubt she did) she became visible, put it back in the locket, and smiled agreeably at me. Naturally, I had a good many questions to ask about

11

this, but you will hardly expect me to put them all down. Becoming invisible in this way was a privilege which the girls always had till they were grown up, and I suppose I may say " came out." Of course, if they presumed on it, the lockets were taken away for the time being—just in the same way as the boys were sometimes stopped from flying, as we have seen. But their own families could always see them, or at any rate the flowers in their hair, and they could always see each other.

But dear me ! how much am I to tell of the conversation of that evening ? One part at least : I remembered to ask about the pictures of the things that had happened in former times in places where I chanced to be. Was I obliged to see them, whether they were pleasant or horrible ? " Oh no," they said ; if you shut your eyes from below—that meant pushing up the lower eyelids—you would be rid of them ; and you would only begin seeing them, either if you wanted to, or else if you left your mind quite blank, and were thinking of nothing in particular. Then they would begin to come, and there was no knowing how old they might be; that depended on how angry or excited or happy or sad the people had been to whom they happened.

And that reminds me of another thing. Wag had got rather fidgety while we were talking, and was flying up to the ceiling and down again, and walking on his hands, and so forth, when his mother said :

"Dear, do be quiet. Why don't you take a glass and amuse yourself with it? Here's the key of the cupboard."

She threw it to him and he caught it and ran to a tall bureau opposite and unlocked it. After humming and flitting about in front of it for a little time, he pulled a thing like a slate off a shelf where there were a large number of them.

"What have you got?" said his mother.

"The one I didn't get to the end of yesterday, about the dragon."

"Oh, that's a very good one," said she. "I used to be very fond of that."

"I liked it awfully as far as I got," he said, and was betaking himself to a settle on the other side of the room when I asked if I might see it, and he brought it to me.

It was just like a small looking-glass in a frame, and the frame had one or two buttons or little knobs on it. Wag put it into my hand and then got behind me and put his chin on my shoulder.

"That's where I'd got to," he said; "he's just going out through the forest."

I thought at the first glance that I was looking at a very good copy of a picture. It was a knight on horseback, in plate-armour, and the armour looked as if it had really seen service. The horse was a massive white beast, rather of the cart-horse type, but not so "hairy in the hoof"; the background was a wood, chiefly of oak-trees; but the undergrowth was wonderfully painted. I felt that if I looked into it I should see every blade of grass and every bramble-leaf.

" Ready ? " said Wag, and reached over and moved one of the knobs. The knight shook his rein, and the horse began to move at a foot-pace.

" Well, but he can't *hear* anything, Wag," said his father.

" I thought you wanted to be quiet," said Wag, " but we'll have it aloud if you like."

He slid aside another knob, and I began to hear the tread of the horse and the creaking of the saddle and the chink of the armour, as well as a rising breeze which now came sighing through the wood. Like a cinema, you will say, of course. Well, it was ; but there was colour and sound, and you could hold it in your hand, and it wasn't a photograph, but the live thing which you could stop at pleasure, and look into every detail of it.

Well, I went on reading, as you may say, this glass. In a theatre, you know, if you saw a knight riding through a forest, the effect would be managed by making the scenery slide backwards past him; and in a cinema it could all be shortened up by increasing the pace or leaving out part of the film. Here it was not like that; we seemed to be keeping pace and going along with the knight. Presently he began to sing. He had a loud voice and uttered his words crisply, so that I had no difficulty in making out the song. It was about a lady who was very proud and haughty to him and would have nothing to say to his suit, and it declared that the only thing left for him was to lay himself down under a tree. But he seemed quite cheerful about it, and indeed neither his complexion nor the glance of his eye gave any sign that he was suffering the pangs of hopeless love.

Suddenly his horse stopped short and snorted uneasily. The knight left off singing in the middle of a verse, looked earnestly into the wood at the back of the picture, and then out towards us, and then behind him. He patted his horse's neck, and then, humming to himself, put on his gauntlets, which were hanging at his saddle bow, managed somehow to latch or bolt the fastenings of them, slipped down his visor, and took the hilt of his sword in one hand and the sheath in the other and loosened the blade in the sheath. He had hardly done this when the horse shied violently and reared; and out of the thicket on the near side of the road (I suppose) something shot up in front of him on the saddle. We all drew in our breath.

"Don't be frightened, dear," said Mrs. Wag to the youngest girl, who had given a sort of jump. "He's quite safe this time."

I must say it did not look like it. The beast that had leapt on to the saddle was tearing with its claws, drawing back its head and driving it forward again with horrid force against the visor, and was at such close quarters that the knight could not possibly either draw or use his sword. It was a horrible beast, too ; evidently a young dragon. As it sat on the saddle-bow, its head was just about on a level with the knight's. It had four short legs with long toes and claws. It clung to the saddle with the hind feet and tore with the fore feet, as I said. Its head was rather long, and had two pointed ears and two small sharp horns. Besides, it had bat wings, with which it buffeted the knight, but its tail was short. I don't know whether it had been bitten or cut off in some previous fight. It was all of a mustard-yellow colour. The knight was for the moment having a bad time of it, for the horse was plunging and the dragon doing its very worst. The crisis was not long, though. The knight took hold of the right wing with both hands and tore the membrane upwards to the root, like parchment. It bled yellow blood, and the dragon gave a grating scream. Then he clutched it hard by the neck and managed to wrench it away from its hold on the saddle; and when it was in the air, he whirled its body, heavy as it was, first over his back and then forwards again, and its neck-bone, I suppose, broke, for it was quite limp when he cast it down. He looked down at it for a little, and seeing it stir, he got off, with the rein over his arm, drew his sword, cut the head off, and kicked it away some yards. The next thing he did was to push up his visor, look upward, mutter something I could not well hear, and cross himself; after which he said aloud, " Where man finds one of a brood, he may look for more," mounted, turned his horse's head and galloped off the way he had come.

We had not followed him far through the wood when—

"Bother!" said Wag, "there's the bell"; and he reached over and slid back the knobs in the frame, and the knight stopped.

12

I was full of questions, but there was no time to put them. Good-nights had to be said quickly, and Father Wag saw me out of the front door.

I set out on what seemed a considerable walk across the rough grass towards the enormous building in which I lived. I suppose I did not really take many minutes about getting to the path; and as I stepped on to it—rather carefully, for it was a longish way down—why, without any shock or any odd feeling, I was my own size again. And I went to bed pondering much upon the events of the day.

Well, I began this communication by saying that I was going to explain to you how it was that I "heard something from the owls," and I think I have explained how it is that I am able to say that I have done so. Exactly what it was that you and I were talking about when I mentioned the owls, I dare say neither of us remembers.

As you can see, I have had more exciting experiences than merely conversing with them—interesting, and, I think, unusual as that is. I have not, of course, told you nearly all there is to tell, but perhaps I have said enough for the present. More, if you should wish it, another time.

As to present conditions. To-day there is a slight coolness between Wisp and the cat. He made his way into a mouse-hole which she was watching, and enticed her close up to it by scratchings and other sounds, and then, when she came quite near (taking great trouble, of course, to make no noise whatever), he put his head out and blew in her face, which affronted her very much. However, I believe I have persuaded her that he meant no harm.

The room is rather full of them to-night. Wag and most of the rest are rehearsing a play which they mean to present before I go. Slim, who happens not to be wanted for a time, is manœuvring on the table, facing me, and is trying to produce a portrait of me which shall be a little less libellous than his first effort. He has just now shown me the final production, with which he is greatly pleased. I am not.

Farewell. I am, with the usual expressions of regard,

Yours,

M (or N).